TEDDY
and
The Birthday Party

Teddy opened his eyes and stretched out in bed.
Today was special, Mummy Bear had said.
The sun shone through on the spot where he lay,
And then he remembered, it was his birthday!

Today he was four, and a party was planned,
All his friends were invited, it was going to be grand.
His guests were asked to be there by three,
And Mummy Bear planned a scrumptious tea.

Teddy jumped out of bed, bounced across the floor,
      Turned the handle and opened the door.
He stood for a while and twitched his nose,
      From below in the kitchen the smell of porridge arose.

Porridge, milk and honey were delicious to eat,
  He ate them each morning, it was always a treat.
He brushed his teeth and washed his face,
  Then ran down the stairs, as if in a race.

addy Bear smiled and said,
        "Happy Birthday, son."
ummy did too, then said,
        "There's no need to run."

e ate his porridge from his own little plate,
        Then ran to the garden to wait by the gate.

Postman Bear was coming,
    With a bag full of post.
Teddy Bear wondered
    If he'd get the most.
"Happy Birthday," he smiled,
    Giving Teddy a bundle.
Then off down the lane,
    He continued to trundle.

Teddy ran inside, as happy as could be,
He wondered to himself, ''Can these all be for me?''
He counted the envelopes, and saw there were ten,
He opened the first — it was greetings from Ben.

There were cards from Granny and Grandad too,
    And nice cards from Bessy and 'Winnie the Pooh'!
There were cards from Buddy, Bobby and Bimbo,
    And another card too, from his little friend Jimbo.

There was a card from Bruno,
　　　Which made him so glad,
And last but not least,
　　　One from Mummy and Dad.

Such lovely cards — so colourful and bright,
　　　He stood them all up — what a wonderful sight!

Mummy Bear said, "There's some shopping to do,
    I'm off to the village, would you like to come too?
We need some bread, tea, cream and honey,
    I have a long list, so I must take some money."

Mummy took a bag,
Covered with green and white spots.
Daddy had a bag,
That would hold lots and lots.
Teddy hurried ahead,
Doing jumps, skips and hops.
And after a while,
They arrived at the shops.

They went to the grocer's,
        For some nice, tasty ham,
Cereals and fruit,
        And a large jar of jam.

Then to the baker's,
        And butcher's too.
The weight of their bags,
        Just grew and grew.

t last they had finished,
　　The shopping was done.
nd homeward they strolled,
　　In the warmth of the sun.

oon they arrived at their little cottage door,
　　And tired arms placed the bags on the floor.

Mummy Bear said, "It's a quarter to two,
      I must get busy, there's so much to do."
She laid the table with cups and plates,
      Then sandwiches, jellies, biscuits and cakes.

Teddy was excited, and shouted with glee,
"Look at the clock, it's almost three!"
Suddenly, with laughter and a hearty roar,
All his friends came through the door.

They sat at the table, such a merry throng,
    And then, all at once, burst into song.
''Happy Birthday to you,'' they sang with delight,
    And Daddy Bear set the candles alight.

Mummy Bear had made a beautiful cake,
      Full of fruit, nuts and flour, and then let it bake.
he icing on top was red and white,
      For Teddy and friends it was a wonderful sight.

After their tea,
        They played lots of games,
Jimbo did impressions,
        And they had to guess names.
They sang and they danced,
        And jumped up and down,
And Daddy Bear came in,
        Dressed as a clown.

They gave Teddy presents, he was so pleased and proud.
He wanted to thank them, and shouted out loud,
''Thank you for coming, we've had such a good time.''
Just then the clock at six began to chime.

His friends said, "Goodbye, it has been a nice day."
They laughed and they joked as they went on their way.
Teddy went upstairs and got into bed,
Plumped up his pillow and laid down his head.
Mummy and Daddy kissed him goodnight,
Tiptoed from his room, and switched off the light.
Teddy had fallen asleep where he lay,
Dreaming, no doubt, of his wonderful day.